Charlie's First Day of School

Andrew Carnegie

HEMINGWAY
PUBLISHERS

SCHOOL

This is Charlie.

This was Charlie's first day
at school.

Charlie had a great day!

First, he went to music class.

He loved to sing.

Next, Charlie went outside to play.

Then, he ate lunch.
He had so much fun!

Next, Charlie learned how to read.

But he was getting tired.

He almost fell asleep!

"No, no, no" said the teacher.

Finally, the last bell rang.

SCHOOL
10

It was time to go home now.

Charlie rode on bus #10

The bus dropped Charlie off
at his home.

Charlie waved goodbye to his
friends and went inside.

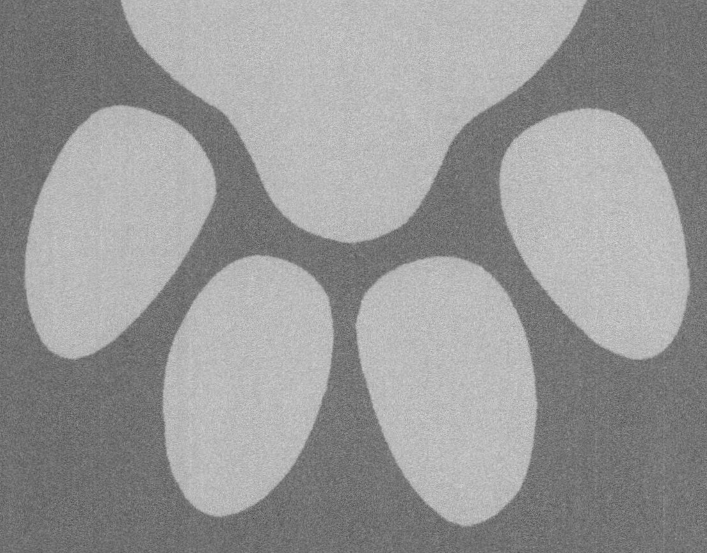

Then he ate some food.

Finally, he fell asleep.

And dreamt about his first day
of school.

THE END !